D1584078

This book contains two funny stories, one of which, *Fiona Finds Her Tongue*, was shortlisted for the Smarties Book Prize.

Diana Hendry is a poet and the author of many stories for young readers, including *Harvey Angell*, which won the Whitbread Children's Novel Award. She has also written the picture books *Dog Dottington* and *Christmas in Exeter Street*, the chapter books *Wonderful Robert and Sweetie-Pie Nell*; *Flower Street Friends*; *Sam Sticks and Delilah* and *Kid Kibble*, as well as the Walker Doubles (two books in one) *Hannah and Darjeeling*; *The Dream Camel and the Dazzling Cat* and *Midnight Pirate, Midnight Party*. She is also the author of novels for older readers, including *Double Vision* and *Minders* and two volumes of poetry, one for adults and one for children. She has a minor talent for spinning plates!

Books by the same author

The Dream Camel and the Dazzling Cat

Flower Street Friends

Hannah and Darjeeling

Kid Kibble

Midnight Pirate, Midnight Party

Sam Sticks and Delilah

Wonderful Robert and Sweetie-pie Nell

For older readers

Double Vision

Minders

CONTENTS

Fiona Finds
Her Tongue

*All through mouthfuls of crunchy Ricicles
and toast, Fiona talked.*

CHAPTER 1

At home Fiona talked and talked and talked and talked.

She talked to her panda, Elias, when she woke up in the morning. She talked to her shoes that stood by the cupboard.

"I'm coming soon, shoes," said Fiona, snuggling down under the blankets.

She talked to the radiator and the radiator talked back. It gurgled and grumbled and groaned about all the hard work it had to do making the house warm.

Fiona talked to her mother at breakfast. All through mouthfuls of crunchy Ricicles and toast, Fiona talked. She talked to the dog,

Stew-pot, and she talked to the cat, Sprogs.

"Stew-pot, you are not having any of my crusts this morning," Fiona would say. "I'm hungry."

And to Sprogs: "Don't you think Ricicles are much nicer than fish fingers, Sprogs?" (But Sprogs stretched a lazy paw and stalked away. He thought it was a silly question.)

And when there was nothing and nobody to talk to, Fiona talked to herself. She talked to herself all the way upstairs to the bathroom. She talked to herself in the mirror. "Well, well, Fiona Bennett. Don't you look a mess this morning!" she said to Fiona-in-the-mirror. "What big eyes you have and what big teeth!" and she stuck her teeth out like the fangs of the wolf in "Little Red Riding Hood".

When Fiona's father came home from work, Fiona rushed to the gate to meet him.

And she talked. All the way up the garden path, all the way into the kitchen and all the way up the stairs. Fiona's father shut himself in the bathroom. Fiona sat outside. And talked.

"She never stops!" said Fiona's mother. "She's more than a chatterbox. She's a gibble-gabble! She's a wind-bag! She's like my seven-day alarm clock! Do you know she even talks in her sleep?" And it was true. Fiona did.

But Fiona did all her talking at home. Outside of Number 21 Victoria Drive, Crouch End, something funny happened to Fiona. She stopped talking. When she went to the shops with her mother, when she went to birthday parties, when she went to tea with her grandma, when she went to visit the doctor or the dentist, Fiona said … nothing.

"Are you going to carry the potatoes for your mum?" asked the vegetable shop lady, and Fiona would clutch the bag of potatoes to her chest and say … nothing.

"Isn't she a shy little thing!" said the lady.

"Would you like banana sandwiches or tomato?" Fiona was asked when she went to a birthday party. And Fiona would try very hard to say, "I would love a banana sandwich and I'd hate a tomato sandwich because of all the slimy, squelchy pips." But nothing would come out. Not even, "Banana, please." At almost every party Fiona ate tomato-and-slimy-pips sandwiches.

"How is my little Fiona today?" her grandma would ask when Fiona and her mother arrived for tea. And Fiona wanted to say: "I'm horrid and cross today and I've got a big scratch on my arm and Daddy won't

Fiona would clutch the bag of potatoes to
her chest and say ... nothing.

let me have dancing lessons and Mummy made me wear this ugghy green T-shirt and I hate it."

But she said nothing of this. She just hid her face against her mother's arm and giggled.

"Don't be silly, Fiona," said her mother, "you're not a baby."

And Grandma said what Grandma always said: "Oh, Fiona's lost her tongue again."

Now Fiona knew perfectly well that she had not lost her tongue because when Grandma had first said this, she had gone to the mirror in the hall and looked. Her tongue was still there, popping in and out of her mouth like a little pink Punch from "Punch and Judy".

But *something* happened to her tongue. It seemed to get very fat and take up all the space in her mouth. It seemed to get jammed between her teeth like a car in a too-tight car-parking place. It curled up inside her mouth (like Stew-pot in his basket when he'd been bad and was scared) and it wouldn't wag.

"Whatever will you do when you go to school?" asked Grandma.

"I really don't know," sighed Fiona's mother, answering for Fiona. And nor did Fiona. Fiona cried about it at night, in bed. She was to start school in a week's time. The teacher would ask her questions. She would expect Fiona to answer them. Other children would talk to her. Would *they* think she had lost her tongue too?

"Whatever is the matter?" asked Fiona's father when he found her curled up in bed making Elias soggy with tears.

"I can't talk!" sobbed Fiona. "How can I go to school if I can't talk? And Grandma

15

says I've lost my tongue. Only I haven't. It's right there inside my mouth," (and Fiona stuck it out), "but it's so crowded with words in there that not one of them can wriggle out."

"Plenty are coming out now!" said her father, stroking Fiona's hair which some called ginger and some called red and some called auburn.

"But that's at home!" wailed Fiona. "My tongue is happy here, it wags quite easily. See," (and Fiona wagged), "it's no trouble at all at home!"

"I have noticed!" said her father, laughing. "Fiona, do you know what I think is the matter with your tongue?"

"What?" asked Fiona.

"Your tongue is like a tap when you turn it on too hard," said her father. "All the water – or the words – come rushing out. Sometimes, when a lot of water has built up in the tank and you turn the tap on, nothing happens. It gives a cough and a splutter and stops. It's so full up with water it can't make a start. Have you noticed?"

"Yes, I have," said Fiona. "My tank has built up such a lot of words inside it that I can't get started either."

"I know," said her father. "I've never known a bigger tank of words in all my life. Listen, tomorrow let's try an experiment. When you are at home just turn your word-tap on a little bit. Say a few words at a time. Then have a rest. Try a little silence, Fiona."

Fiona stared at her father in amazement. "And you think that will work? You think that will get my tongue to wag the way it ought to wag?"

"I think it very well might," said her father, tucking her in.

"I'll try it!" said Fiona and she folded her lips tight as if she were practising silence.

CHAPTER 2

The next morning Fiona did not talk to Elias and she did not talk to her shoes (although she gave them a wave so that they would know they were not forgotten).

At breakfast she was just about to tell her mother what an odd thing it was that her radiator not only gurgled and grumbled and groaned at her, but it also *winked*! The early morning light rippled along the ridges of the radiator and the radiator winked. Now wasn't that odd? And Fiona tried to wink back but it was very difficult because…

Fiona was about to say all this but then she stopped. She had caught her father's eye.

Her father grinned and put his finger to his lips in a "Ssshhh" sort of way.

Fiona took a big gulp of air, turned her tap of words until it was just going ker-plop-plop-plop, and said, very carefully, "My radiator winked at me this morning."

"How do you mean, winked?" asked Fiona's mother. She suspected a joke.

Fiona took another gulp of air and turned her tap on just a little bit more. "All its crinkly edges went glint, glint, glint," said Fiona and skidded to a full stop the way Stew-pot did when he rushed down the stairs too fast and met the front door.

"Oh, I *see*!" said her mother at once. "As *if* it were winking."

Fiona nodded. (Today she wasn't even going to waste a "yes".)

Fiona's father, ready for work, kissed the top of her head and whispered, "Well done!"

For the rest of the morning it was very quiet at 21 Victoria Drive, Crouch End. "Do you feel all right?" Fiona's mother asked her. "You're very quiet today."

"I'm looking after the tap," said Fiona.

"That's nice, dear," said her mother, who was busy making a cake for Grandma.

Fiona wanted to say that it wasn't at all nice and however did Stew-pot and Sprogs and the flowers in the garden manage without words? But she didn't. Perhaps, thought Fiona, people were born with different kinds of word-taps like they had different types of noses.

When she had made the cake, Fiona's mother called Fiona upstairs.

"I want you to practise tying your shoelaces for school," said her mother. They sat on the floor together and Fiona's mother made a loop of lace.

"That's the tree trunk," said Fiona's mother.

Fiona said nothing.

Her mother made a loop of the second lace.

"That's the rabbit," she said.

Still Fiona said nothing.

"And here goes the rabbit round the tree trunk and up the hole under the tree," said Fiona's mother. "And there's the bow!" And she pulled the two laces tight in a nice, neat bow.

Now there were a great many things Fiona wanted to say about the rabbit and the tree. How, she wanted to ask, was she to know which lace was the rabbit and which the tree? Could she colour the laces, perhaps, with her Pentels? One lace green and one lace yellow, and then she would remember. She wanted to say that a shoelace made a

Fiona's mother pulled the
two laces in a nice, neat bow.

very skinny rabbit. She wanted to ask if the bow, when it was made, was meant to be the rabbit's ears popping out of the hole.

Fiona practised silence for such a long time that her mother felt her forehead to see if she was getting chickenpox like Alice-down-the-road.

At last Fiona turned her word-tap to allow just the tiniest drip. "Rabbit's ears!" said Fiona.

"What?" asked her mother, startled.

Fiona pointed to the bow and said again, "Rabbit's ears."

"Oh, I *see*," said her mother. "The bow looks like the rabbit's ears sticking out of the hole. Well, you have a practise while I get things ready to go to Grandma's."

What a lot of practising, thought Fiona, but she sat on the floor and made the rabbit shoelace run round the tree shoelace. She didn't talk to the rabbit. She didn't talk to the tree. She didn't talk to her shoes and she didn't talk to herself. And there was no fun in it. It was very dull.

By the time Fiona's mother was ready for Grandma's, there were so many words in Fiona's word-tank that she thought she might burst. The words gurgled and groaned and grumbled inside her just like the hot water in the radiator getting hotter and wanting to rush through the pipes.

Fiona's mother walked slowly. She did not want to shake the chocolate cake in its tin. At last Grandma's house was in sight! Fiona could bear it no longer. She rushed up the path, burst in the back door and she opened her mouth to let all those lovely warm words go running about Grandma's house.

Fiona was about to say: "Grandma! Grandma! I'm going to school tomorrow!

I can tie my own shoelaces and make the rabbit run round the tree. And Alice-down-the-road has got chickenpox."

That is what Fiona *wanted* to say. But then the awful thing happened. She opened her mouth and nothing came out. Not a word. Her tongue was in a traffic jam between her teeth. Her cheeks went scarlet. Tears came to her eyes.

"Oh dear," said Grandma, as Grandma *always* said. "Fiona's lost her tongue again." And then Fiona's tank did burst, not into words, but tears.

"I think Fiona is a bit upset today," said her mother, arriving with the chocolate cake safe in its tin. "She starts school tomorrow, you know."

"I know," said Grandma. "I've bought her a present." And she went to the cupboard under the stairs, where she kept her surprises, and she brought out a large square parcel wrapped in green tissue paper with a big gold ribbon tied in a rabbit's ears bow.

When Fiona opened it she found it was a scarlet leather school satchel with shining silver buckles and a little see-through pocket in the front where she could write her name and address.

"Ooooh, Grandma!" cried Fiona, forgetting all about taps and tanks and silences. "It's the most beautiful satchel I've ever seen!"

And Grandma laughed and said, "Just listen! Fiona's found her tongue!"

Then Fiona blushed as red as her hair and lost her tongue all over again!

"Oh," cried Fiona to her father when she and her tongue were safely home again and he was sitting on the edge of her bed at bedtime. "However am I going to get my taps just right?"

"I think you've made a very good start," said her father. "After all, you did manage to say *something* to Grandma and Mummy tells me you've practised a lot of silence at home."

"But it's the Off, On, Off, On part I can't manage," said Fiona. "What will happen at school if my word-tap is Off when it should be On and On when it should be Off?"

Fiona's father thought for a moment.

"Listen," he said, "I've got a magic little something that I'm going to put in your satchel so that you can use it if you really get stuck for words. Right?"

"Right," said Fiona.

Then her father wrote something on a piece of paper and "posted" it in the pocket of Fiona's satchel.

Fiona fell asleep and dreamed that her

satchel was a talking satchel and whenever the teacher asked her a question the satchel answered for her.

*On that first morning at school Fiona's
word-tap was stuck.*

CHAPTER 3

But of course the satchel didn't say a word.

And nor did Fiona!

On that first morning at school Fiona's word-tap was so stuck that even if you were the biggest, strongest plumber in all the world you could not have turned it on.

"Now," said the teacher, sitting at her desk, "every morning I take the register. That means I have a list of your names here and I read them out and when I call *your* name, you say, 'Yes, Miss'. That's so I know you are all here and nobody's missing. We'll do it slowly this morning so that I can get to know all your names."

And off she went:

Amanda? Yes, Miss ✓ (whisper)
Thomas? Yes, Miss ✓ (giggle-and-squeak)
Jane? Yes, Miss ✓ (loud-and-brave)
Rowena? Yes, Miss ✓ (pianissimo)
David? Yes, Miss ✓ (dolce)
Fiona?

"FIONA? FIONA? FIONA?"

Fiona's name seemed to echo round the classroom like a bit of "hot" running all round the pipes. Fiona dug frantically in her satchel for her father's magic-something, for if ever a magic-something was needed, now was the moment. She pulled out the piece of paper. Her father had drawn a picture of Fiona and in the picture Fiona wore an enormous smile. At once Fiona smiled. She smiled so wide she thought she'd come to the end of her cheeks.

The teacher looked up and saw her. "Oh, there you are, Fiona," she said. "I expect you've lost your tongue this morning. We all feel rather shy on the first day."

There were twenty-four children in Fiona's class and twenty-two of them said, "Yes, Miss."

"Tai?" called the teacher, ticking her way down the register. "Tai?" And there was a silence just like Fiona's silence only when Fiona looked round to see who owned this silence, she saw that Tai didn't have a red satchel with a magic-something in it and Tai's silence wasn't a smiling silence, it was a sad silence. Two tears were about to slide down his nose.

But the teacher saw Tai's tears just as she had seen Fiona's smile. "Well, children," said the teacher, "this is Tai. He comes all the way from Vietnam so I don't suppose he knows much English yet. We must all try to help him."

Fiona looked at Tai in horror. *She* knew what it was like to lose her tongue, to be stuck for words. But to have an empty word-tank or a tank full of words that nobody else could understand … well! Not one word, not twenty words, could say how awful that must be.

For the first lesson the children were to do some painting. Fiona took a palette of paints from the cupboard over to the table which the teacher had spread with newspapers and set out with yoghurt pots full of water. There were lots of brushes standing in jam-jars like bunches of hairy flowers.

Fiona found herself sitting next to Tai.

"I want you all to paint me a picture of your own house," said the teacher, "with the garden if you want to."

Fiona took a pencil and began to draw 21 Victoria Drive, Crouch End. She drew a square, four crooked windows (with Sprogs in one of them), a door with a very big letterbox and a garden path lined with speechless flowers.

Tai stared at his empty piece of paper. It was as empty as his word-tank. All he could colour it with was two more tears.

And then, as if someone had applied just a very little oil to the stiff washers of Fiona's word-tap, Fiona found her tongue.

"House!" said Fiona to Tai, pointing to her own picture. "House!" she said again.

Tai looked at her. He had a fringe of silky black hair and eyes that shone like the glossy school piano in the big hall.

"Owss?" said Tai.

"House!" said Fiona.

Tai and Fiona giggled so much that the teacher came to see what was going on.

"Owss!" said Tai. But he picked up his pencil and began to draw.

But Tai did not draw a house. He drew a boat.

"No," said Fiona, pointing to his picture. "Boat. Not house. Boat." And then pointing from his picture to her picture, "Boat, house, boat, house."

"But, owss, but, owss," said Tai and they both giggled so much that the teacher came to see what was going on.

When she saw Tai's picture of a boat she said, "I expect Tai's home has been a boat. You see, when there was a war, Tai's family lost their house and they spent months and months sailing to England in a boat. I expect a boat means home to Tai."

"But!" said Tai, spotting this one word out of all the others the teacher had used.

The teacher laughed. "Oh, well done, Tai!

You're learning English fast. Thank you for being so helpful, Fiona."

But Tai was busy drawing as fast as he could. He drew four windows, a door and a chimney. "Owss!" said Tai, beaming and pointing to the new picture. And, "But!" said Tai, pointing to the first picture.

"This is a house," said Fiona, pointing to Tai's "owss", "BUT this is a boat," pointing to Tai's "but".

"But," said Tai.

"Boat," said Fiona and they both burst out laughing again.

And after that Fiona's word-tap went Off and On just when she wanted it to and by the time Tai went home to his "owss" he had four new English words and one new English friend. The words were HOUSE (owss), BOAT (but), YES (yuss), NO (nuh) and the friend, of course, was Fiona (Nona).

When Fiona's father came home from work that evening, Fiona rushed down the garden to meet him. "Daddy, it was all right!" cried Fiona. "My tap worked! I thought it was stuck for ever but then I met Tai and Tai didn't have any words at all so I had to give him some from my word-tank. And now he's got four new words!"

"So I suppose you didn't need the magic-something in your satchel after all?" said her father.

"Oh, Daddy, I did, I did. Right at the beginning, when I wanted to say 'Yes, Miss' and nothing would come out. *Then* I needed it."

"Did it work?" asked her father.

"It did!" said Fiona. "Miss knew at once who I was without my saying a word."

"You don't always need words," said Fiona's father.

"No," agreed Fiona, "but they're nice to

have around, aren't they?"

"And so are you!" said her father, giving her a hug.

"I know another magic-something," said Fiona, "something just as magic as smiles."

"What's that?" asked her father.

"Tears," said Fiona. Then her father took her hand and they walked up the path together without saying a word. And that was a magic silence.

Fiona Talks
to Herself

*That morning, in the middle of winter, was like
no other morning.*

CHAPTER 1

One morning in the middle of winter, Fiona woke up and, as usual, began talking.

"Morning, Elias," she said to her panda, as she always did. "Time to wake up."

But that morning was like no other morning.

"I'm already awake," said Panda. "I've been awake for hours. In fact, I didn't sleep a wink all night."

Fiona was almost dumb with astonishment. Almost.

She picked Elias up and shook him gently.

"What?" she said. "What did you say?"

"I said I didn't sleep a wink last night and

45

please could you not shake me up like that," said Elias.

"I'm very sorry," said Fiona.

"I should think so," grumbled Elias. "And now, if you don't mind, I'd like to go back to bed. I'm feeling rather delicate today."

"Yes, of course!" said Fiona, tucking him in. "Can I get you anything to make you feel better?"

"Some pyjamas would be nice," said Elias. "And maybe you could get your mother to knit me some clothes? How would you like to be naked all winter?"

"I wouldn't like it at all," said Fiona. "But doesn't your fur keep you warm?"

"As fur coats go," said Elias, "mine is rather thin."

"I suppose it is," agreed Fiona. "I'll see what I can do."

"Pyjamas and a nice stripy jersey," said

Elias, and went to sleep.

Fiona put on her own stripy jersey and her jeans, then she pulled her shoes out from under the bed.

"Good morning, shoes," said Fiona, as she always did.

But that morning was like no other morning.

"What's good about it?" asked Left Shoe.

"Dull!" said Right Shoe. "We're both feeling very dull."

"And if you wouldn't mind," said Left Shoe, "we'd really like some clean socks today."

"Oh!" said Fiona. "Yes, of course. I've got some new yellow socks. Maybe they'd make you feel brighter?"

"Yellow's my favourite," said Right Shoe.

"I prefer blue, myself," said Left Shoe. "But yellow will do for today."

47

"Perhaps you'd like a polish?" suggested Fiona.

"Thought you'd never ask," said both shoes together, and they flapped their tongues at her and wriggled their laces.

"It is rather a long time since you had one," Fiona admitted, putting on her new yellow socks.

"Two weeks come Thursday," said Left Shoe.

"And if you could avoid the puddles today, I'd be most grateful," said Right Shoe. "If there's one thing I can't stand, it's a damp sole."

"I'll be very careful," said Fiona as she prepared to carry them downstairs, one in each hand. But just as she was leaving the room, the radiator gave a cough and a gurgle.

Now Fiona was used to radiator language.

The radiator spoke in gurgles and grumbles and groans when it was warming up and creaks and "eeeks" when it was cooling down. But it didn't usually use *words*!

But that morning was like no other morning.

"Lo-lo-lo-lo-lonely!" said the radiator with a sigh. And then with another gurgle, "Always left a-lo-lo-lone!"

Fiona stopped and gave the radiator a pat. Then she ran her hand gently along its ridges.

"Oooooh!" said the radiator. "That's nice! Do it again!"

So Fiona did.

"I'm sorry you're lonely," she said. "But I'll be back later. Would you like a T-shirt and perhaps my pyjamas to keep you company?"

"Ummmm!" said the radiator. "Keeping

them warm will give me something to do all the long lo-lo-lo-lonely day."

So Fiona laid a T-shirt and her pyjamas over the radiator, and giving Elias a quick kiss, went downstairs with her shoes.

"I wonder who else will talk to me today?" Fiona asked them.

"Fiona? Is that you talking to yourself again?" asked her mother.

"Not exactly," said Fiona.

The shoes chuckled. Very quietly.

Fiona sat down at the breakfast table. Stew-pot came to sit beside her. He rested a paw on her knee. Then Sprogs climbed out of her basket, stretched a paw, licked her whiskers briefly, and strolled across the room to sit on the other side of Fiona.

"Leave us a few crusts, there's a pal," said Stew-pot gruffly.

"And leave me a little milk to lick," said

50

Stew-pot came to sit beside Fiona.
He rested a paw on her knee.

Sprogs as Fiona added milk to her cereal.

"Crusts make my tail curl," said Stew-pot.

"Milk keeps my whiskers white," said Sprogs.

Fiona looked at her mother to see if she had heard Stew-pot and Sprogs talking, but Mrs Bennett was drinking her tea and looking at the newspaper.

"Stew-pot wants my crusts," said Fiona. "And Sprogs would like some milk."

Mrs Bennett laughed. "I suppose they've just told you that, have they?"

"Yes," said Fiona, "they did. I think I'll polish my shoes today. And do you think you could make Elias some pyjamas and perhaps knit him a jersey? A stripy one like mine. He says his fur is a bit thin for winter."

"He does, does he?" said Mrs Bennett. "Well, I'll see what I can do. Has anyone else been talking to you this morning?"

But Fiona didn't like to tell her mother about the radiator and the shoes. She took the shoe polish and a brush from the drawer, sat on the floor and began polishing them.

"Ooh! Ah! Ooh!" said the shoes.

Fiona looked across at her mother, but Mrs Bennett didn't seem to have heard anything.

"Perhaps," Fiona whispered to the shoes, "I've got magic ears!"

The shoes wagged their tongues at her.

Just then the doorbell rang.

"Hurry up, Fiona," said Mrs Bennett. "That will be Tai and his mother. It's their turn to take you to school today."

"Hurry! Hurry! Hurry!" whispered the shoes.

Fiona put them on quickly, grabbed her coat and satchel and gave her mother a kiss.

"See you later darling-oh," said Mrs Bennett.

Fiona ran out of the door and slammed it shut behind her.

She was halfway down the path and saying "hello" to Tai and his mother when she heard the letterbox snap, "See you later, kid!"

CHAPTER 2

As if they were now quite happy, the shoes stopped talking when Fiona walked. She was careful to avoid puddles so as not to upset Right Shoe.

Tai, who could now speak English easily, chattered away about a TV programme he had watched the night before. But that morning, which was like no other morning, Fiona wasn't listening to Tai, because suddenly there were so many other voices to listen to.

Fiona's satchel, for instance. They were only halfway down the road when the satchel began humming quietly to itself and then it burst into a little song:

>"*Jiggledy joggledy,*
>*Books and pens,*
>*Five plum puddings*
>*And two red hens,*"

sang the satchel, jiggledy jogging on Fiona's shoulder.

"Don't be silly," said Fiona. "I know you're carrying my sandwiches but I'm quite sure you haven't got five plum puddings and two red hens."

>"*Jiggledy joggledy,*
>*Wait till you open me,*
>*See what I hide in me,*
>*I've a surprise or three*
>*In the inside of me,*
>*Jiggledy joggledy,*
>*Jolly-dee me!*"

sang the satchel.

"Jiggledy joggledy, books and pens, five plum
puddings and two red hens," sang the satchel.

"You do feel rather heavy," said Fiona.

"Who are you talking to?" asked Tai.

"Myself," said Fiona quickly.

"When Tai's at school, I talk to myself a lot," said Tai's mother.

"And do things talk back to you?" asked Fiona.

Tai's mother laughed. "I'm afraid not," she said.

"Sometimes the wind talks to me," said Tai. "It says 'whooosh' and 'whish-ish-ish' and 'woo-hoo-hoo.'" And Tai went running and whooshing down the road as if he was the wind itself.

Tai's mother ran after him. Fiona plodded slowly behind them, pulling up the hood of her coat for it was a very cold morning.

"All gone! All gone! All gone!" said a mournful voice.

Fiona looked about her.

"All gone!" repeated the voice. Fiona felt something tickle her cheek. It was the little twiggy branch of an oak tree.

"What's all gone?" asked Fiona.

"My leaves, of course," said the tree. "And I miss them. I miss them badly."

Fiona gave the tree a quick hug. "They'll be back," she said. "Really they will."

"Are you sure?" asked the tree sounding more hopeful.

"Quite sure," said Fiona. "In the spring you'll have lovely new leaves. Don't you remember last spring?"

"I can remember long ago," said the tree, "but I can't remember yesterday or last spring. New leaves, you say?"

"Yes," said Fiona, "Like a brand new dress."

Tai and his mother had stopped at the newsagent's.

"I'm just buying Tai a drink for lunch-time," called Tai's mother.

Tai waited outside the shop and practised hopping. Fiona began to run so that she could do some hopping too, but she had only run a few paces when a voice said, "I do think that's awfully rude. Running past me like that, without even a 'good morning'."

"I'm terribly sorry," said Fiona to the postbox. "I didn't notice you standing there."

"Didn't notice me?" said the postbox. "Me, in my brightest red coat?"

"I'm very sorry," said Fiona again.

"I'm not sure if I should tell you my important news," said the postbox.

"Please do," said Fiona.

"Come closer then," said the postbox.

Fiona bent down so that her ear was on a level with the postbox's mouth.

"I've a letter in me from James Carey to Elizabeth Lewis telling her he loves her," said the postbox.

"Gosh!" said Fiona.

"And I've a letter from Mrs McNally that's going all the way to India. I've got Mr Bright's gas bill and a letter from Sally Brown to her pen friend in America and somewhere down the bottom I've got a letter from Tom Coleman thanking his aunt for his birthday present. It was socks, you know. She always sends him socks but this year…"

"I'm awfully sorry to interrupt," said Fiona (who had begun to think that the postbox would never stop talking), "but I've got to get to school."

"Oh well then," said the postbox huffily, "if you don't want to know…"

"But I do! I do!" cried Fiona. "You're twice as interesting as any school lesson."

"Thank you," said the postbox. "If I wasn't already red I might blush. Off you go then. Send me a letter sometime, will you?"

"I will! I will!" promised Fiona and she ran to join Tai and his mother, who were waiting for her outside the shop.

"Quarter to nine. Please be on time," said the church clock as they all walked past.

"Quarter to nine," said Tai's mother looking up at the clock as if, thought Fiona, it hadn't said a word. "We'd better hurry."

They reached the school gate just as the bell was chanting: "Come on in. Time to begin."

Tai's mother waved goodbye to Tai, and Fiona ran down the path and into school.

But for Fiona it was a school day like no other!

To begin with, when she changed her shoes for her trainers, the shoes grumbled at being put in the locker.

"I suppose you don't know how boring it is in here," said Left Shoe.

"And dark," added Right Shoe.

"I'm very sorry," said Fiona (who began to wonder if she was to spend the whole day saying "sorry"), "but it's school rules to wear trainers indoors. Perhaps you could go to sleep?"

"Want to go walk-about," said Left Shoe.

"Want to go run-skip-hop-and-jump-about," said Right Shoe.

Fiona shut the door on them firmly.

She had a peep into her satchel and was pleased to find there was a surprise inside her lunch box – two jam tarts and a satsuma.

> *"Hang me up on your peg*
> *And I'll sing to myself,"*

sang the satchel.

Fiona did as she was told. It was lucky that everyone else was too busy chattering to hear the satchel singing.

And then it was Assembly and Fiona didn't hear what Mrs Pitts, the headmistress, was saying at all because she was busy listening to a robin who sat on the window-sill.

"Teachers," said the robin, "do so much talking I can't make myself heard." And it went off into a long song about winter and snow.

"That was very nice," whispered Fiona.

"Somebody's whispering," said Mrs Pitts. "Please stop!"

"See what I mean?" said the robin and flew away.

At lunch-time, standing at the serving hatch, Fiona could quite clearly hear the cook's pans talking to each other. They

"Teachers," said the robin, "do so much talking
I can't make myself heard."

rattled and chattered and gossiped away.

"Well," said the big potato pan, "I told Teapot that I was fed up with her moaning all the time."

"She has a cushy life," said the small custard pan.

"That's just what I said. I said, 'I must be honest with you, Teapot, your working hours are nothing like ours! And you're everyone's favourite,' I said. Honestly, I was *steaming*!" And the potato pan rattled its lid crossly.

"You told her all right," said the small custard pan. "Have you heard about the wooden spoons? Such goings-on last night!"

Fiona was dying to hear about the goings-on of the wooden spoons, but the dinner lady interrupted.

"Move along, dear," she said. "You're holding up the queue."

Out in the playground after lunch Fiona was about to join in a skipping game when a voice said, "I say, over here a minute!"

At first Fiona couldn't see who – or *what* – was speaking.

"Pssst!" said the voice again. "Over here!" And Fiona saw it was the school caretaker's broom, leaning against the wall.

"Want to know about my dream?" asked the broom casually.

"Oh, yes please!" said Fiona.

"I was invited," said the broom, "to sweep out the rooms of heaven."

"Good heavens!" said Fiona. "I mean, gosh!"

"*And,*" said the broom, "if I say it myself, I did a very nifty job. There was a great deal of star-dust to be shifted."

Fiona was about to ask the broom to tell her more about his dream when she heard

Jem Atkins behind her. Jem was one of the bigger boys.

"Fiona's talking to herself again! Talking to herself!" sang Jem.

"I am not!" shouted Fiona. And then stopped. For how could she tell him she was talking to the caretaker's broom? How could she tell anyone?

CHAPTER 3

Fiona was glad when it was going-home time.

"Thought you were never coming!" said Left Shoe.

"Can we dance home?" asked Right Shoe.

"I don't feel much like dancing," said Fiona.

"She's at it again!" called Jem. "Fiona's talking to herself."

Fiona's father, home early from work, came to collect her. Tai was off to the dentist. His mother came for him in the car.

Fiona and her father began walking home.

"Half past three! Time for tea!" sang the

church clock as they walked past.

"I hope Mum's got the kettle on," said Fiona's father, just as if he had heard the clock speaking.

Fiona looked at him curiously. "Did the clock tell you it was time for tea?" she asked.

"Well, it didn't exactly *tell* me," said her father. "But maybe seeing the time put the idea into my head that a cup of tea would be nice. And something else tells me that you've got a problem."

"What sort of something else tells you that?" asked Fiona.

Fiona's father stopped and laughed. "I suppose it's the look on your face," he said, "a kind of worried look."

"Things have been talking to me all day," said Fiona. "First Elias, then my shoes and the radiator. Then Stew-pot and Sprogs – why even that postbox spoke to me this morning." And Fiona pointed at it standing stiff as a soldier on the corner.

"Let's see if it's got anything to say now," said Fiona's father. So they marched up to the postbox and Fiona bent her ear to its mouth.

"Ab-so-lu-te-ly full!" said the postbox.

"Well?" asked her father.

"It said, 'ab-so-lu-te-ly full'," repeated Fiona.

"I suppose it is," said her father. "It's just about time for the postman to empty it."

"But you didn't hear it speak!" said Fiona.

"No," said her father rather sadly, "I seem to remember that when I was a child lots of things spoke to me, and then as I grew older they stopped."

"Oh!" said Fiona more happily.

"There were particular days – rather magical ones," said her father, "when the world seemed to be talking to me and I was talking to the world." He sighed. "One day I went fishing," he continued, "and the river spoke to me."

"What did it say?" asked Fiona.

"It said, 'Come from far, far away'," said her father. "Then I caught a fish and the fish spoke too."

"What did the fish say?" asked Fiona.

"It said, 'Put me back! Put me back!'"

"So did you?"

"Yes, I did," said her father.

"I think maybe I've had one of those magical days," said Fiona as they walked past the old oak tree.

"Another day," whispered the tree very faintly. "We'll talk another day."

When they got home Mrs Bennett had made a pot of tea and a mug of milk for Fiona.

There were biscuits too and Stew-pot, hoping for crumbs, came to sit beside Fiona. But he didn't speak. Sprogs strolled past, but she didn't speak either.

"I've been very busy today," said Fiona's mother and she opened her sewing bag and held up a pair of pyjamas and a stripy jersey – with just the same stripes as Fiona's. "For Elias," she said.

Fiona rushed upstairs and grabbed Elias from the bed.

"Look, Elias!" she said, "Lovely new pyjamas and a stripy jersey just like mine!" And she dressed him in both. He looked very grand.

"You might at least say, 'thank you'," said Fiona. But Elias only smiled.

Fiona remembered the tree whispering "another day, another day". Perhaps there would be another day, another magical day,

"Let's go downstairs and see if there are any
biscuits left," said Fiona to Elias.

when Elias would talk again. She gave him a hug.

Fiona took off her shoes and put on her slippers.

She waited a while to see if the shoes had anything to say for themselves, but the shoes sat side by side and said nothing.

The radiator gave a nice contented gurgle and then fell silent. It was a good, comfortable sort of silence, Fiona thought.

"Well," she said, picking up Elias, "if you're not going to talk to me, I shall just have to talk to myself. Let's go downstairs and see if there are any biscuits left."

So they did. And there were.

THE

END

THE BEST DAY OF THE WEEK
by Hannah Cole

For Angela and her older sister Carole, the best day of the week is Saturday. That's the day they (and Angela's bear Fergus) go to visit Granny and Grandpa in their house by the river.

These warm-hearted stories tell of three very different but unforgettable Saturdays: a happy, rainy day of hopscotch, a sad day at the hospital and a magical day at the theatre with a pantomime witch.

WILLA AND OLD MISS ANNIE
by Berlie Doherty

This book is about a little girl called Willa and her friend Old Miss Annie. When Willa first meets Miss Annie, she is afraid of her, because of the old lady's woolly hair and her tiny voice and her bumpy, twisted hands. But now they are the best of friends. One of the things they have in common is a great love of animals, as you will discover in these three warm and enchanting stories – featuring a goat, a pony and a fox – by double Carnegie medallist Berlie Doherty.

MORE WALKER STORYBOOKS
For You to Enjoy